T0072412

Loopa and the Earth Crocs

Loopa and the Earth Crocs

AVINASH SEN

PARTRIDGE

A Penguin Random House Company

Print information available on the last page.

To order additional copies of this book, contact
Toll Free 800 101 2657 (Singapore)
Toll Free 1 800 81 7340 (Malaysia)
orders.singapore@partridgepublishing.com

www.partridgepublishing.com/singapore

Dedications:

I would like to dedicate this story to my mum and dad
and my good friends at Arena multimedia
Sougat
Mouktik
Pushkar
Asif
Riya
Sampurna
Pranjali
Paul
Subhajit
And anyone else I may have forgotten
They showed surprising interest in this story as I wrote this
and it's thanks to that I had the motivation to continue
writing this and other stories thanks guys.

CHAPTER 1

Sandcastle

The earthquakes had started again. Thankfully, Loopa was outside playing when it started this time, a lucky break after a really long time. But it was still annoying for Loopa. She had been making a nice sand castle when the earthquake hit.

This always happened when she was having fun. It was bad enough when the tent almost caught fire that time, a few days ago. Did the earthquake have to destroy her nice sandcastle too? Yes, it was only half done, but that wasn't the point.

Perhaps an explanation is in order. As you can probably tell, Loopa is the centre of our story. She lives in a small village which goes by the name "Sanclatony," which is in the middle of the desert, but they have at least seven oases nearby, so it isn't too bad.

The village used to be filled with nice, sturdy houses made of bricks and wood. That was, of course, before the earthquakes started.

They struck once or twice every few days; they were very unpredictable. The only saving grace was the fact that, although they were long (one once lasted for seven minutes), they weren't intense. They didn't have any way to measure them so they weren't sure about the intensity part.

When the earthquakes had first started, the villagers tried making stronger houses, but they didn't have the resources. So, eventually, they took to living in tents. True, they fell very easily, but, at least they provided shelter, and most importantly, they didn't hurt you if they fell on top of you. It had been like this for years, well before Loopa, the little heroine of our story, was even born. Most people had become used to this, even Loopa.

But, the thing was that she didn't want to be used to it. Her grandmother used to tell her about the times before the earthquakes. The nice sturdy houses they had, no fear of something hurting you, no fear of falling even when your feet were on the ground. She wished so strongly for these things, it was like Loopa was the one who lived through the non-earthquake period, not her grandmother. She remembered one time, long ago, when she asked her grandmother what exactly caused the earthquakes.

That was when she first heard about the earth crocs. They were crocodile type creatures whose skin reflected the earth they lived in. The desert crocs were sandy, the rain forest crocs were marshy and the wasteland crocs looked like cracked, dry earth. They moved about the world underground, only coming to the surface every now then to check how things were. They usually lived by themselves, but that didn't mean they didn't move in groups now and then. It was this moving of a group of earth crocs that caused earthquakes on the surface.

Grandma used to say that earth crocs must have built something like a new station or cross roads underneath the village and it was this which caused the earthquake epidemic in the village. At first, Loopa believed in this story, thinking it was a fine explanation, indeed. But as time went by, after talking with her friends and neighbors, she believed it less and less, until that particular belief disappeared completely. But, although she didn't believe in the earth crocs any more, she did wonder about the cause of the earthquakes. What had changed between then and now, between before the earthquakes started and the very first earthquake?

She knew that something had happened and she wanted to know what. She wanted to know if she could change things back to the way they were. She was going to find out, and she knew how.

She had a plan.

—⟋⟋—

CHAPTER 2

Crockery and Cutlery and What-Not

Once the earthquake was over, she stayed where she was for a little while just to make sure - then she ran back to her tent of a home, remembering her promise to her parents.

"Loopa darling, whenever an earthquake strikes, after it is over and if you're not hurt, you're to come home immediately and show us you are fine. Or else we'll assume you're hurt, or worse, you hear me. I don't care if you are playing with your friends or not. You come straight here."

She hadn't broken that promise yet, but part of her plan involved breaking it later. So better build up some kudo points now.

Although it was hot, she ran as fast as she could. After all, running on dry sand was pretty hard, try it some time, you'll see what I'm talking about. She could see her tent on top of the next dune, it didn't look like the earthquake had done too much damage this time.

But that was outside. It could be a completely different story inside.

She walked the rest of the way, she was pretty tired now. Inside the tent things weren't that bad; that's not to say they were completely okay.

One of the vases had fallen over and cracked, two or three pictures had fallen and one of the chairs had fallen over too. All in all, not too bad.

"Mama, Papa!" said Loopa, obviously calling her parents.

"In here darling."

Loopa followed the voice, it sounded like it came from the kitchen. She should have known. The stove. If an earthquake knocked that over there would be a fire; her parents must be checking and making sure. When Loopa went into the part of the tent which served as the kitchen, it was obvious that things were worse off here than anywhere else.

While nothing had burned or caught fire, the stove had upended. Unfortunately the upended stove had hit their cupboard full of crockery and cutlery and what-nots. Some of the stuff had made it but a lot of it was broken beyond repair. The water jug, the pots of pickle, a lot of the plates….but what really got to Loopa was when she saw the state of her mother's favorite ceramic plate. It was just a clay plate, like the others, but it was ingrained with different slices of stone, making beautiful flower and plant patterns. Now most of the stone slices had come off and there was a big spider-web crack smack in the middle. That plate had made it through all the earthquakes which hit it. Her mother had told her it was their good luck charm, saying if the plate could make it they could make it. And now *this* happened.

It didn't make much difference to Loopa, but it did make a difference to her mother. You could see it in her face, and the way her hands jerked slightly when she was picking up the pieces. This really made Loopa sad; the earthquake had taken a lot of things from them, but when the plate had broken, it had taken a little bit of her mother's happiness along with it. Loopa's mother saw how sad Loopa was after seeing the plate and went to hug her little girl.

"Don't worry honey, it's only a plate. We can make another one." Loopa wanted to push her mother away and shout at her, telling her that it was not okay, that they shouldn't have to suffer like this.

She came pretty close, too. But she didn't; instead she just hugged her back.

The plan, the plan. The plan will make things better, the plan will help them all, the plan will make all this sadness a bad memory. She was banking a lot on the plan. She hoped for her own sake and everyone else's sake that it would work.

"Don't worry, Mama, I know that it's just a plate. I'm not sad, really."

Her father was picking up some of the plates and spoons which were still intact. Then he set them on the table, went up to Loopa and Mama and smiled. "It isn't as bad as it seems. Yes, a lot of the crockery is broken, but a lot is still left, and I'm sure we can fix the stove in no time."

That was her Father, always looking at the bright side.

Loopa looked up at him and smiled, but inside she was sad. This was supposed to be his day off from work, he was supposed to be relaxing, but the earthquake took even that away from them. Of course, their family wasn't the only one suffering, but that was beside the point. If anything, it was all the more reason to make things right again, or at least try to.

A little fun facts, trivia and history before we continue the story, if you don't mind, and even if you do.

The village of Sanclatony had three main means of earning a living: pottery, merchant trading and mining, the last being <u>the</u> main source of income. The mine was situated approximately 20 kilometers away from the village. It was originally closer, but the noise from the workings of the mines made it 'difficult' if nothing else, to live nearby. The old houses were used as headquarters for the mine workers and also as living quarters of sorts. The mines themselves had quite a collection of metals and minerals, diamonds, rubies, gold, iron, silver, copper, zinc and other things you've never even heard of. More than half the village worked at the mines, including Loopa's father.

There were also little furry creatures called "Fuzzywumps" who were about three feet high. They worked together with the human miners to help get to the hard to reach spots. Their village was also near the mine but in the opposite direction. It's the fuzzywumps who inspired Loopa's plan.

You see, Loopa's plan, which included some friends who thought like her, was to go to the mines, disguise themselves as fuzzywumps, sneak in, go as deep underground as possible, find out and possibly fix the problem.

It was a stupid plan, I know, but they were desperate and they were kids. What did you expect from them?

Getting to the mines was going to be easy enough. Loopa's father was due to go back to work there, so the caravans would be coming to pick him up along with the other workers. They were going to ride underneath the caravans, shoved between the beams. There wasn't enough space for a grown-up to think about fitting there, but they were kids, so it was ideal. Once they got to the mines they would have to pretty much play it by ear.

And now, back to the story.

It has now been a few hours since the earthquake. Things have been cleaned up as best as they can be for now and the tent looks to be in better shape. It is about four o'clock now (or what passes as four o'clock in that area. Time was different there, they didn't have o'clock's). So Loopa thought it was safe to ask her parents if she could go out for a while. "Mama, Papa, is it okay if I go out to visit my friend?"

"I don't know honey," said her father, "it's getting a bit late now."

"Awww! Please! Just because there are earthquakes doesn't mean I can't have fun. Besides, I'll be very, very careful."

"Let her go, darling," said her mother, "she's right, she should have some fun, now more than ever, I reckon."

Loopa's father looked at his wife, then his daughter, then his wife again. Slowly he began to yield.

"All right, Loopa, you can go."

Loopa ran up to her father and gave him as big a hug as she could; she even gave him a kiss on the cheek, just to show that she loved him. Then she ran out of the tent as if he might change his mind.

"But remember the rule," shouted her father from the cloth door, "if another earthquake hits, you are to come straight back here once it's over. Do you hear me, Loopa?"

"Yes Papa, I will, I promise," shouted back Loopa, running all the time.

As I mentioned before, Loopa's village used to be a proper one with stone and wood buildings. I also might or might not have mentioned that now it was just a collection of tents placed around a big oasis (forgive a writer for his absent mind). There wasn't any particular order to the placement of these tents; they were just wherever the families wanted to put them up.

Outside each tent was the family sigil and beneath that the family name (some families insisted on writing their names in the old tongue, and this annoyed the kids especially, because they hadn't learned to read in the old tongue yet).

Loopa went to collect her various friends.

Caprica (one of her best friends, born almost on the same day as Loopa if not for a few minutes).

Jason (another good friend, not as close as Caprica, but still.)

Blayt (a rather recent friend. They'd known him before, but they only became good friends a couple of months ago).

And finally, Selena (Blayt's younger sister; she had been playing with Loopa long before him. In fact she was the one who introduced Blayt to her friends).

Loopa had gone to their houses in that order to call them to come to their meeting place in the outer oasis. But it had turned out that Blayt had already gone there and taken Selena with him. It always seemed like he knew when some major decision was being made. He was odd that way; he boasted that he had strong intuition or something. When Loopa, Caprica and Jason got to the oasis they saw Blayt up a date tree collecting dates and Selena below him catching dates as he threw them down.

"Loopa," shouted Selena as soon as she saw them. Selena always considered Loopa the leader of their group, so naturally, when she called out to Loopa she was calling out to the rest of them too, she just didn't say their names.

"Hi everybody, would you like a date? Brother said you would all probably come here, like he 'knew' again." This she said with a little irritation; as I said before, he liked to boast about his intuition.

"I also said that we'd find some good dates here," shouted Blayt while climbing down from the tree. The group decided to eat their dates and ignore Blayt for a while, they'd been through this before, they knew how to deflate Blayt's ego.

"Oh, come on. You're going to do this to the boy who is giving you the dates, after doing all the hard work!"

They ignored him some more, enjoying the dates, making faces at each other.

"Okay, so have you decided *when*, Loopa?"

They knew this was just Blayt's way of making them talk, so they ignored him for a little longer. But not too long, they all wanted to know if Loopa had decided when.

She threw away a date seed and swallowed what was in her mouth

"We're going tomorrow, when our parents leave for the mines."

All of them widened their eyes and looked at each other, waiting for someone to say something. No one did, they were all ready.

That isn't to say they didn't have questions. Selena raised her hand.

"I'm not a teacher, Selena; you don't have to raise your hand."

She kept her hand up.

"Okay, Selena, what is it?"

"How do we sneak in, again?"

"We'll have to wake up early so that we're the first when the caravans come. Then we hide in between the beams under them, we should be able to fit."

"We're not going to end up going round and round while we're going?" asked Selena.

Loopa giggled a little at this. "No, don't worry, we won't go round and round. Anyway, after that we'll have to get off and find some straw and the fuzzywump uniforms so we can disguise ourselves. We'll have to be sneaky or else we'll get caught and, by Hayloth, we don't want that! After that we get into the mines and solve the problem. Any questions?"

This time Jason raised his hand.

"What is it, Jason?"

"Well …"

"What is it? Spit it out."

Jason was acting flustered about something, whatever it was. It was almost like the dates didn't agree with him.

"Well… It's just… are you sure about this, Loopa?"

Silence.

"I mean, this is going to be pretty dangerous, they don't allow kids at the mines for a reason, we might get hurt. Badly."

More silence from the group. Then Loopa put on a face, a pretty scary face.

"Well, Jason, would you rather your parents and family get hurt *because* of the earthquakes? Would you rather *our* families got hurt?"

Now Loopa was really getting into Jason's face, and boy, was he starting to feel small.

"Well…uhh, if you… put it that way…"

Loopa saw how scared and sorry Jason was and immediately changed tack.

"Look, Jason, I understand you're scared. But it's this or putting up with the earthquakes forever."

Silence from Jason.

"Jason, life's hard enough without the earthquakes. Why should we put up with them when we *can* get rid of them?"

Jason slowly looked up at Loopa. "Do you really think we can do this?"

She went to hug her friend and ruffle his hair; it seemed to perk him up a bit. "Of course we can, Jason. Now let's play and enjoy ourselves. We've got a big day ahead."

"I want to play hide and seek."

"No, let's play sand-worms versus rock-moles."

"But we played that yesterday."

"How about King of the Sand dunes?"

And so the children played long after the sun set and had as much fun as they possibly could. After all, they wouldn't be able to play tomorrow.

—⟳—

CHAPTER 3

Caravans and Fuzzywumps

Speaking of tomorrow, it was already upon them … evening had come and gone, the friends had gone home, bodies tired from all the playing, hearts light from the fun, but heads heavy for the future and what might come.

They slept, sometimes dreaming of success, sometimes of failure and sometimes of something else altogether (now those parts were really funny!).

But back to the story.

It was about 4.30am when Loopa woke up. She got up and stuffed her pillow under her blanket to make it look like someone was still in the bed. Then she began tip-toeing her way out of the tent. There was a bit of a scare when, in the dark (the sun had not risen yet,) she bumped into the giant vase which had fallen over during the earthquake. The thing wobbled a lot, but luckily, didn't fall. She stayed still for a while to make sure no one heard her. When no one called, she decided it was safe to leave.

It took her a while but eventually she made it to the caravans' stopping place.

The caravans weren't here (they wouldn't be till 6.00) and neither were her friends. Where were they? They must've overslept. Loopa thought about going to get them but that was too risky, she might get caught. She decided to wait for them; if worse came to worst she would leave on her own, she was not giving up just because of this.

Time passed by and Loopa was really getting impatient and anxious. It had just crossed her mind that they hadn't thought of a place to hide before the caravans came. How were they going to sneak onto the caravans if they were caught now? The caravan guards would definitely ask questions, not to mention that it was already suspicious that a child was up so early in the middle of the desert of all places. But even that wasn't as worrisome as why weren't her friends here yet.

Were they still asleep? Would they wake up too late? Were they all caught somehow, or had Jason's talk got to them all and they had chickened out without telling her? Ooh, if that was the case she was going to kill them once this was over. She would rip them to shreds, she would tear them limb from limb, she would …

"Loopa, hi Loopa!" shouted Caprica from a distance. She was coming along with the rest of them.

By golly, was Loopa relieved, but she wasn't going to show them that!

"What. In. Hayloth's. Name. TOOK YOU SO LONG?"

All of them froze in front of Loopa's fierce stare. In fact they all looked very much like Jason had when Loopa had talked to him about chickening out. Then Caprica started to explain.

"We *are* sorry, Loopa, but none of us have woken up so early before. Not to mention that Selena fell asleep while getting here and Blayt had to carry her all the way." Selena was rubbing her eyes and trying to look sorry. Caprica always did try to be the practical one, although this time it didn't look like practicality would win out. Loopa seemed P.R.E.T.T.Y. angry!

"I've never woken this early either, why can't you?" shouted Loopa. "You are an exception Loopa," said Caprica calmly. Caprica's calm seemed to have gotten through to Loopa. Though she still looked angry, you could see that in her frown, but the frown was less intense now. "Well, you are here now and that does make things better," said Loopa. "Glad you see it that way!" said Caprica, smiling with relief. All of them were more relaxed now; it was never pretty when Loopa got mad.

But something did still seem to trouble her.

"What's wrong Loopa?" asked Jason.

"I just realized we have no place to hide before the caravans get here."

This news made them all widen their eyes, no one wanted to get caught, that was for sure. Everyone started looking around to find a good place to hide, they didn't have much time.

"We could go over that dune and sneak back when they come," said Caprica.

"Uhh, guys …" this was Selena. She was fully awake by now.

"We could just say we came here to play," said Jason.

"This early in the morning? I don't think so. If there were only some bushes around here, then we could hide behind them."

"Loopa," said Selena again.

"Instead, all we have is sand. Too bad we're not earth crocs, then we could just burrow beneath the sand."

"LOOPA!"

'What is it, Selena?"

"The caravans, they're coming!"

There, out in the distance were the caravans, coming straight for them. They were coming fast.

"Quick, up the sand dunes now."

"Are you crazy? We'll never get up there in time!"

"If we run fast, we just might make it."

"But they will definitely see us when we're coming back. Uff!" A handful of sand hit Jason full in the face. He looked around and saw Blayt doing something strange. "Uh, Blayt, what are you doing?"

"Just help me, quick, I have an idea!"

—w—

The caravans (which looked like square tents on wheels) had reached their destination. They were a strange lot, one was driven by horses, one by donkeys and one was driven by a strange new contraption built by the local inventor. He called it a "steam engine," whatever that was supposed to be. The wheels were strange too. They were made out of rubber and had slits through which flaps could come out to help when the vehicle was trapped in the sand. It looked something like this:

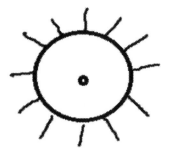

But the most interesting were the drivers, or rather, what they were saying. They were arguing about something.

"I'm telling you I saw people standing here just a few minutes ago."

"Are you sure it wasn't a mirage?"

"The sun hasn't even come out yet."

"Maybe you're not getting enough sleep."

"I'm *not* falling asleep on the job."

"Then you're probably going mad!"

"I'm not going mad!"

"Then how come there's no one here?"

"How am I supposed to know? But they were here, I saw them."

"Then why didn't we see them?"

"Well, I've always had better eyesight than yours."

"Oh, not that again!"

While this interesting discussion was going on, five lumps of sand suddenly started moving near the caravans. Guess what they were? Go on, guess!

Well, anyway, when these lumps reached the caravans (the underneath, that is) the lumps broke and five children popped out, shaking the sand from their hair and clothes. Said Loopa, whispering, "that was a pretty good plan, Blayt, how did you come up with it?"

"You gave me the idea, when you mentioned the earth crocs," Blayt whispered back.

Things were a bit easier after that. They quickly scrambled beneath the caravan supports, hurriedly adjusting themselves so that they would get as comfortable a ride as possible. They arranged themselves like this: Caprica and Selena to one caravan, Jason and Loopa to another, and Blayt alone on the steam engine one. Now all they had to do was wait.

Time dragged on, the sun eventually came up, and soon after, the workers started arriving, getting ready to leave.

"Finally. I began to think they would never come," said Loopa.

And then, once the caravans were full, they began their long journey to the mines.

It was pretty rough travelling like this, all things considered. Every now and then the spinning wheels threw sand in their faces, they were jostled around and whenever the wheels hit a large stone they would jump up and come back down with a big, painful bump. "Ouch! That one really smarts!" said Loopa. "If I land up not being able to have children of my own, I'm blaming you!" said Jason.

"How can you blame me?" asked Loopa.

"Well, it was your idea to use the caravans. Couldn't you have gotten a better idea?" said Jason.

"Oh, and how, pray tell, would *you* have gotten us to the mines?" asked Loopa sarcastically.

"…and then we found out my wife's favorite plate was broken," said a voice sadly.

"What did you just say?" asked Loopa.

"That wasn't me," whispered Jason.

After a while, they realized it was coming from the caravan. The people inside were obviously talking. It might interest you that they also realized that this particular person was Loopa's father.

"Now, that is just sad, my friend," said another voice. This turned out to be Jason's father.

"But at least your daughter is still safe," said Jason's father (from here on to be referred to as JF.)

"I thank the stars for that small mercy every day," said Loopa's father (to be referred to as LF.)

"You know, it seems like just yesterday that Loopa was just a little baby, barely bigger than my arm. Now look at her, growing up so fast, it's sad sometimes," said LF.

"I know how you feel," said JF. "Ha, ha, I remember when Jason was about three years old. He would wet his bed every single night! Drove my wife mad sometimes since she ended up washing clothes at night."

Well, quite obviously, Jason was embarrassed. Loopa started chuckling. Want to guess why?

"Please stop laughing, Loopa," said Jason, very red in the face. She didn't stop laughing.

"Loopa, I swear I won't be friends anymore if you don't stop, right now." She did stop, but anyone could see she still wanted to laugh. Her mouth just wouldn't stop twitching. "So. What are you going to do to make sure I don't tell anyone about this?" said Loopa.

Then LF started talking. "That reminds me of when my Loopa was four years old, I told her a ghost story one day, to pass the time. After that, for a month she would wake up screaming in the middle of the night and come running to our bed, crying about how the fuzzywump with fangs was coming to eat her!'

It was now Loopa's turn to turn red.

"Hmmm, I think blackmailing you with what *I* just heard might stop you from talking about what *you* just heard," said Jason.

"Alright, alright, maybe I was a bit harsh on you. How about we both forget what we heard and move on?"

"Agreed."

"Hmm, that was pretty bad! But I remember this one time with Jason …"

"Oh no!"

Needless to say it was a very long journey, and not just because of the distance.

By the time it was over, Jason and Loopa looked either like really juicy tomatoes or overcooked human lobsters, take your pick.

Once the three caravans stopped, they waited for everyone to get off, using the dust raised from their feet and the sound of people talking to cover their getting off and hiding. All of them looked and found a good hiding place behind a pile of supply sacks. The first to make it to the sacks were Loopa and Jason, then Caprica and Selena and finally, Blayt.

Before they even caught their breaths Selena started talking.

"That was so exciting; we were like real spies, assassins sneaking into the castle to kill the Evil King!"

"It did go off better than I thought,' said Caprica. "We got on the caravans fine, thanks to Blayt, there wasn't *that* much sand coming on our faces and Selena actually enjoyed herself!"

"Whenever I started getting really bored I pretended the beams were horses and I was going around in stealth mode, the beams were going up and down like real horses and..." it was only then that Selena got a real good look at her other companions. Loopa and Jason were still red with embarrassment and Blayt was completely black from head to toe.

"What happened to all of you?" asked Caprica and Selena together.

"We don't want to talk about it," said Loopa and Jason, also together.

Then they all stared at Blayt and let their faces ask the question for them.

Blayt coughed some smoke out and then answered, "let's just say I don't want to ever do that again. Ever! Too much smoke and oil for my taste!"

All of them (except for Blayt) had grins on their faces after getting a good look at Blayt. (Loopa and Jason were feeling much better). Blayt gave them all his best baleful stare. It would have been scary if he hadn't looked so funny!

All of them (except Blayt) got a good chuckle in before they got serious again. Then Loopa started planning. "Okay, Blayt's situation aside (you're gonna have to tell us how that happened to you!), we have to find fuzzywump uniforms for ourselves, not to mention, some straw. Anyone know where the uniforms are kept?"

Everyone shook their heads.

"Hmm, I was afraid of that. Okay, we'll split up into four teams. Jason, you take the north side, Selena, you take west, Blayt, you go with Selena, Caprica will take east and I'll..."

"Why don't we just follow those fuzzywumps over there, they might lead us to the uniforms," said Caprica. Sure enough, three fuzzywumps were heading in the easterly direction, chatting among themselves.

"That'll work," said Loopa. "Okay, change of plan. Caprica, you come with me, we'll follow the fuzzywumps and get the uniforms, the rest of you go find some straw. We'll meet back here. Got it?"

Everyone nodded

"This is just like how the spies in the stories do it!" said Selena in excitement.

"That's true Selena, but don't lose your head, we don't want to get caught," said Blayt.

"Okay everyone, let's go. Good luck!"

And they were off.

Now, for simplicities sake, I'm only going to follow Loopa and Caprica for a while; but don't worry, I'll tell you what happened to the rest of them later, just not in so much detail.

Now, the thing about fuzzywumps is that they are like moles. They don't use their eyes that much; they use their feet and hands to feel the vibrations around them, and their ears to hear sounds. They also use their noses, but not as much. This made following a fuzzywump undetected very difficult. They almost always know if there's danger nearby, but that's not to say they are perfect. For instance, the three fuzzywumps that Caprica and Loopa were following were talking to each other about something, almost forgetting their surroundings completely, making things easier for the followers.

At first Loopa and Caprica were worried that they would be spotted and were really tense. But they relaxed a bit later when they began to realize the fuzzywumps weren't paying attention. They realized this when one of the fuzzywumps walked right into a wall when his friend turned (poor little guy).

So, with not that much stealth (they didn't need it), they followed the fuzzywumps.

It took a while (the fuzzywumps kept bumping into walls) but eventually they got to the place where the fuzzywumps kept their uniforms.

As soon as the three fuzzywumps came out (now in their uniforms), Loopa and Caprica went in. It took them quite a while to find five uniforms which fit. Jason, Caprica and Loopa were all more or less the same size but Selena was much smaller and Blayt much taller than them. They would have to do some guesswork. Some of the uniforms were too small, some much too big. Now that was surprising!

They did find some uniforms for themselves and they also found one which would probably fit Selena (they weren't really sure) but finding a uniform for Blayt was proving hard. In the end they just picked the largest they could find and hoped for the best. They'd already spent too much time just searching; if it turned out too big they'd just stuff more straw.

They went outside, each carrying some uniforms, already wearing their own. It was only when they came out of the building that they realized something. They had no idea how to get back to the supply sacks. They were lost!

"Oh, this is just great," said Loopa.

"Now, now. I'm sure we'll be able to find our way back," said Caprica. "Let's just walk around a bit."

"And what if we meet someone?"

"We'll just lower our helmets to cover our faces. Besides, not many people know fuzzywump (that's the language name). All we have to do is make some fuzzywumpish noise."

"What if we come across more fuzzywumps?" asked Loopa.

"Let's worry about that later, okay?" said Caprica.

"Hmm...okay, let's get going,"

They did seem to have been making some progress ("I'm pretty sure we take a left here") but it was still taking them some time.

Loopa decided now was as good a time as any to ask a question which had been bugging her for a while. "Caprica?"

"Yes?"

"Why are you doing this?"

"Doing what?"

"Going through with this?"

Caprica stopped in her tracks and gave Loopa a puzzled look.

"What do you mean? I'm doing it to help the village. Just like everyone else."

Now Loopa looked flustered. "I know, but that's just a base reason. We're all doing this for our own reasons too."

Caprica was silent.

"I'm doing it for *my* family, Blayt and Selena are doing it for each other (that's pretty obvious) and Jason... well, I'm not sure why he's doing it yet and I don't know why you're doing it either."

Caprica was still silent.

"Well... I just wanted to know, that's all."

Loopa started walking again but Caprica stayed where she was.

"Caprica?"

She was still silent. Then, "Loopa, did you know I was going to be a big sister?"

Loopa stayed quiet. A story was coming, a private one, and if she knew one thing, it's that you don't interrupt personal stories.

"It was a few months ago, my mother was pregnant. I was really excited. Now I'd be able to feel how Blayt feels with his sister. See if it was exaggerated or real." (Blayt did go on about how great it was to have a little sister). "But then one of the earthquakes came, Mom fell on her belly. She fell hard… there was blood pouring out from her… my father called it a miscarriage. Needless to say, I was sad, but my Mom and Dad were devastated. It hurt them, it hurt very badly."

Caprica was starting to cry now. "They both said they would never try for a child again, they never wanted to go through that hurt again."

Loopa was completely shocked. "Why didn't you tell me Caprica?"

"My parents didn't really want anyone to know, so I didn't tell. Sometimes things shouldn't be said, not until it's time. But that's why I'm doing this Loopa, I'm hoping for another person in the family, I'm hoping to change my parents' mind. I'm also doing it for that baby that couldn't come. If reincarnation is real, maybe that baby will come back once it's safe."

Loopa immediately went and hugged her best friend.

At first Caprica didn't do anything, and then she hugged back. "As for Jason, I think he's doing it because all his friends are doing it and he thinks it's brave and noble. Also, he probably doesn't want to miss out on an adventure of a lifetime!"

After that they started walking again, this time hand in hand.

CHAPTER 4

Winfela shimpu aksterintoome

While Loopa and Caprica were talking and walking, Blayt, Jason and Selena were trying to do three things at the same time:-

1. Look for enough straw to get the job done.
2. Find a way to haul the straw back to the meeting point.
3. Try not to get caught.

Points one and two were, luckily, easy to fulfill. Not only did they find the straw, but the straw was already stuffed in a wheelbarrow. Convenient, wasn't it? There was a snag though. Although the straw was light the wheelbarrow was pretty heavy. It took both Blayt and Jason to move the wheelbarrow around. Selena decided to go in front and navigate. Now we come back to point number three.

Lugging a heavy wheelbarrow around is hard, but lugging it trying to avoid getting caught is harder. After lots of "take a left, now right, stop, stop, STOP. OKAY, GO! Wait, go back, GO BACK!" from Selena, they finally made it back to the supply sacks. After all this, Jason and Blayt were pretty irritated. And waiting for Loopa and Caprica was making them more irritated.

"Where ARE they?" said Jason.

"I hope they didn't get caught," said Selena.

"They're probably lost," said Blayt.

"Well, they'd better get unlost quick," said Jason.

Loopa and Caprica did get back to the supply sacks eventually, only to be met by an irritated Jason and Blayt.

"Where *were* you guys?" demanded Jason.

"We got lost," said Loopa.

"Told you so," said Blayt.

"Huh, did you at least get the uniforms? Apart from the ones you're wearing?" asked Jason.

"Right here," said Caprica, lifting the arm holding the uniform to show her point. "What about you guys, did you get the straw?"

Blayt, now a little less irritated, showed them the wheelbarrow.

"That looks heavy," said Loopa.

"It was,' said Jason.

"Well, alright then, let's get to it."

Thankfully for most of them, the uniforms were a good fit and they only had to put a little bit of straw to fill in the gaps. But Blayt's uniform was far too big for him and they had to put a lot more straw. And when I say a lot, I mean a *lot*.

"I feel like a fuzzywump scarecrow," said Blayt.

"You *look* like a fuzzywump scarecrow... with eyes," said Selena with a grin on her face.

"As if the steam engine wasn't enough! Remind me to kill you guys when this is over! I can barely move in this thing."

They all looked pretty serious when he said this. They didn't want their plan to fail because Blayt couldn't move.

So Caprica decided to assess the situation. "Okay, let me see you bend your elbows and knees as far as you can." Blayt moved them, barely. "Now bend yourself forward as far as you can." He did this too, with the same results.

"Okay, I think you're good. Let's go everyone!" said Caprica.

"Hey, wait! What do you mean I'm good, I can barely move, hey, come back here. Hey!"

But they wouldn't listen, leaving Blayt to wobble his way to them. If you looked at his friends closely, you could see that all of them were grinning now, if only slightly.

Loopa took the lead and everyone else walked behind her, or in Blayt's case, wobbled. So they walked and walked, took a right, walked, took a left, walked, headed straight, etc, etc.

After a while Jason decided to ask, "uhh, Loopa, you *do* know where we're going, right?"

"Of course. We're headed towards the mines."

"And you know where the mines are, right?"

Now Loopa started slowing down. "Umm... yeah...about that..."

"Oh great! Do you mean to say we've been wasting our time, just walking around?"

"Hey, I *will* find my way, just be patient."

"Be patient! This was *your* plan Loopa, and you never thought of PLANNING ahead?"

Now Loopa stopped completely. She was pretty angry. "You're the one to talk! You didn't WANT to come in the first place."

"Yes, and now you can see one of the reasons why."

"Would you rather our parents suffer?"

"Don't bring that up again, that's beside the point."

"That is the entire point."

"Oh sure, that's just your failsafe. Every time someone disagrees with the plan, you immediately come back to that."

"Well, at least I care. You, on the other hand, don't seem to bother whether anyone gets hurt. So stop being such a crybaby and let us do what we have come for."

"How can I not be a 'crybaby' when you are such an incompetent leader?"

"Oh, you are such a..."

"WHAT'S GOING ON HERE?"

Loopa and Jason immediately shut up when they heard this. And the others who were staring at the shouting match immediately regained their senses.

All of them began looking around, trying to find the source of the voice which interrupted them. It was only then that they noticed a figure coming towards them. Judging by the uniform and big pick-axe she was carrying, it was another miner (a human one, by the way).

And yes, you read right, it was a she. I did mention that women worked in the mines too, didn't I? If I didn't, I apologize.

Anyway, so the miner started walking towards them with a stern look on her face. "What are you fuzzywumps doing here? Shouldn't you be working in the mines?"

They all just froze in fear and panic. All of them knew what they should do, but each of them was scared they would mess up. Luckily, Caprica was able to gather her wits quickly enough and started talking fuzzywump, or at least pretending to.

"Winfela shimpu aksterintoome. Shipken toofla semp."

'Well, at least one of you can talk, too bad I can't understand you."

All of them breathed a sigh of relief at this. They all made a mental note to thank Caprica later.

"But I think I know what's going on here."

Now they tensed up again. She hadn't seen through their disguises, had she?

"You small fellows are slacking off, aren't you? Make it easier on yourselves, so 'fess up!"

Thank Hayloth, she hadn't seen through them. They all nodded, trying to look a bit ashamed at being caught.

"Well, can't say I don't understand. What with the danger of being buried by an earthquake. But if we humans can risk our lives, so can you."

They just kept nodding.

"Okay, all of you are going to the mines to work. I'll take you there myself to make sure you don't slack off again. Come along!"

Now they just couldn't believe their luck! Here they were, lost, and out of nowhere a guide comes to help, even if she didn't realize it! It was almost as if Hayloth Himself wished them success.

They eagerly followed the miner, but not too eagerly, they had to act as if they didn't really want to go to the mines and work some more.

While they were walking, they whispered to each other so that the miner couldn't hear. "Well, I must say this is a big stroke of luck," said Blayt.

"Yes, now at least we know where we're going," said Caprica. "At this rate we might just fix the earthquake problem in, well, no time!"

And before they knew it, they were there.

They were in front of the main mine entrance and, by Hayloth, it was HUGE! The entrance by itself was about 10 meters high and 5 meters wide. What's more, the inside was at least 1 to 2 kilometers long. The floor was riddled with what looked like rail tracks, and on each rail track were at least three mining carts, each with its own miniature steam engine attached, to help it move (seeing this brought a scowl on Blayt's face). The walls of the cave were filled to the brim with ledges, stairs and small mine shafts and entrances reaching almost all the way to the ceiling. And out of almost every entrance was another rail track going further and deeper in. It was a precarious structure and a real sight to behold.

This was the first time Loopa and the gang had ever even seen the mines, so they spent some time gaping open-mouthed at the sheer hugeness of it all. They were knocked back to their senses by the voice of the miner calling them.

"What are you little guys doing? Get moving, the rocks aren't gonna mine themselves you know."

All of them realized that the miner had gone deeper into the cave and they were just standing where they were, looking stupid. They all made their way in, lickety split.

"Okay now, let's see. Right, you and you," she pointed at Loopa and Blayt. "See those carts? Their engines need repair, and until they can get fixed, the two of you have the lucky job of moving them to the entrance and emptying them out."

Oh dear! This didn't look good. They hadn't planned on having to do mine work, they thought they would just get to the mines and move on. Looked like every gift had its price; maybe they could slip off once the miner left.

"The rest of you are going to take those pickaxes," she pointed at a wooden stall with pickaxes leaning on it, "and go to that mound of boulders," she pointed at the huge pile of rocks, "and pick out any precious metals you can find. There, I've given you guys some easy jobs to do so don't complain. And don't think of slacking off again either. I'm going to stay right here and keep my eye on you, just to make sure."

Now things were more complicated. How were they going to get out of this situation? Each of the group looked at the other as discretely a possible, hoping someone had an idea about what to do next.

"Well, what are you waiting for, an invitation? Get moving, chop - chop." This last bit was punctuated with the miner clapping her hands twice when she said chop - chop.

It was then and there that each of them realized that there was no way out of this. They would just have to do the work and hope the miner got bored soon, or had to leave for some other reason.

Grudgingly, each of them went to their assigned tasks. It was going to be a long day.

Push, unload and repeat; push, unload and repeat. The words 'grueling work' didn't even cover half of what poor Loopa and Blayt had to go through. You have to remember they were just kids and they had never done this kind of heavy lifting before. And they couldn't stop either, not while the miner had her eyes on them.

Selena, Caprica and Jason were no better off. For them it was: pick, pick, heave–ho; pick, pick, heave-ho, broken by the occasional checking for precious metals.

"This... huff, huff, is...huff, huff... brutal," huffed Loopa.

"I know... huff... what...huff, huff...you mean," huffed Blayt. "And to think...huff, huff... our parents...huff... do this... huff, huff... every day!"

'Un...huff... believable!" said Loopa.

Meanwhile, back with the boulder pickers.

"This is..." heave... "back breaking," said Caprica.

"I think my back is already broken," said Jason.

"You know, that lady hasn't done anything but stare us. I think she's using us as an excuse not to work," said Selena.

"Can you blame her?" said Caprica. "If I had to do this every day, I'd find any excuse not to work."

Then the miner lady started shouting. "Hey, you guys hauling the carts, speed up, you're going too slow! And you! The little one by the rocks. You just tossed a perfectly good piece of gold. Pick it up! Honestly, the way you fellows behave, it's like you've never worked in the mines before!"

"Shucks, I wonder why?" whispered Jason to himself.

Needless to say, the poor friends worked for what felt like hours, or was it days? Thankfully, after what was actually just one hour, they were saved, not by a person but by a noise.

Brrrroooom, brrrrroooooom, brrrrrrrooooooom.

"What was that?" asked Blayt.

"Don't know," said Loopa.

'Well, there goes the lunch horn," said the mean miner lady. "You fellows can take a break now, and have whatever it is you fuzzywumps eat for lunch. I'm going to get some nice stew. But you guys better be back here long before I am, and you'd better be working! A miner's work is never done! And before you start insulting me behind my back, remember, first of all, *you* were in the wrong for slacking off, and secondly, if anyone else had caught you, you'd be out of a job right now, or made to do even harder work than this easy stuff I gave you, so consider yourselves lucky. Well, I'm off. Remember, be back before I am, and work hard!" And with that long and unnecessary speech, the mean miner lady finally left them alone.

"Finally she's gone! I hope I never see her again!" said Loopa.

"I second that!" said Blayt.

"I third and fourth it!" said Selena.

"... I don't know. It was a lot of hard work, but I found it oddly fulfilling, like I was a small part of a larger whole," said Caprica.

This statement was met with bewildered stares from all her friends.

"What? It's just how I feel," said Caprica.

"Okay, never mind that. Right now let's move on to what we really came here to do," said Loopa.

"Right," said the rest of them together.

"Alright, now, a few weeks ago my Papa told me that the miners had found a new and interesting mine shaft hereabouts. He said it was interesting because of all the precious metals it held and also because of how deep it went. Like it went on forever, and more. I say that mine shaft is probably our best bet. We go in as deep as we can, find out what's causing the earthquakes, and stop them."

"One question. Do you know which mine shaft we have to go into?" asked Jason.

"Of course I do! Sheesh, I'm not stupid!"

'Okay then, which one is it?" asked Jason.

"Yes....ummm..."

"Here we go again!" said Jason, exasperated. "See, this is what I was afraid of. What kind of a person makes a plan but doesn't *plan* ahead a little?"

"Get off my case, Jason. Let me think!" said Loopa. "Right, it was a new shaft and I remember my Papa telling me that new shafts have a sign outside them saying something."

"What do they say?" asked Caprica.

"They say 'Do not... Do not'..."

"Do not enter?" asked Blayt.

"No, no. Well yes, but more than just that," said Loopa.

"Do not enter without permission from Mineshaft Manager?" asked Selena.

"Yes, YES! That's it! How did you know that, Selena?"

"It says so on that sign beside that shaft over there," said Selena, pointing.

They turned to look towards where she was pointing, and wouldn't you know it, there was a mineshaft with a sign beside it saying, "Do not enter without permission from Mineshaft Manager."

'Well, okay then," said Loopa.

Now came the moment of truth. Would all of them really, willingly go inside and risk their lives on the small, and I repeat, SMALL chance that they would save their village? Loopa knew *she* would. But what about the others?

"Well my friends, this is it. If any of you are even *thinking* of turning back, then say so now, because you won't get a chance once we're in there."

She looked at each of them, hoping against hope that they would come with her. She didn't want to have to do this alone. Then Caprica spoke up.

"I'm going down there, Loopa. You know very well what I have had to experience because of the earthquakes. If there is a way to stop them, I'm going to."

Loopa smiled at Caprica, she knew she could count on her!

Now Blayt spoke. "My sister and I have suffered a lot because of the quakes. I *am* going to stop them."

"I go where my brother goes," said Selena.

Now only Jason was left. He was always against the plan from the start. If anyone was likely to turn back, it was him. The question was, would he? Loopa for one thought he might, and felt very sad. Jason was one of her best friends, and if he were to go against them now, what would become of that friendship? Jason was just staring at the ground, as if in shame. This didn't look good.

But then he looked up and looked at Loopa straight in the eye and said, "Well, despite what I think of the plan, I do want the earthquakes to end. So I'm in. Besides, what kind of friend abandons his friends, especially when they are doing something this good!"

Loopa immediately gave Jason a hug after he said this, much to his surprise. She was happy and relieved.

"What was that for?" asked Jason.

'Nothing," said Loopa, smiling.

After that, all of them took off their fuzzywump uniforms and kept them in a pile next to the shaft. They kept the helmets though; safety first, after all. Also, the helmets had mini-lanterns on them to help the miners see in the dark.

Now they all faced the opening of the shaft. Adventure awaited them.

'Well, this is it," said Loopa.

And, as one, all of them stepped into the shaft and began walking downwards.

After just a few minutes they came up to another sign which said "Unexplored! Do not enter!" Of course, they ignored it and moved on.

The unexplored part of the mine shaft basically seemed to go even further down. It was filled with dripping stalactites and wet stalagmites. It was a good thing that they had brought the helmets along because it was completely dark, and the dampness made the ground very slippery. One wrong step and they were done for. Also, some of the stalactites were so low; they were in constant danger of knocking their heads, except for Selena, whose small size was finally coming in handy. In fact the others were jealous of her, which was a first!

Although they were being as careful as possible, they still got scraped and cut by the sharp rocks. But all this was nothing compared to a more pressing problem.

By now, they had been walking in the semi-darkness for hours, and they realized they had made one big mistake. They hadn't brought any food or water and all of them were getting very hungry and extremely thirsty. Caprica, luckily, had come up with the idea of using their helmets to collect the water dripping from the stalactites and drink that. They had all jumped to the idea and that was what they were doing right now. But stalactites only go drip, drip, drip, not whoosh, so collecting the water was taking a while.

"Why is it taking so long?" whined Selena.

"Just be patient, Selena, we'll all quench our thirsts soon."

But just thinking about drinking water made them more thirsty. Selena started making a lot of whimpering noises, and in the state her friends were in, they were just about ready to do anything to shut her up. Seeing this, Blayt went up to Selena to try to calm her down a little.

"Look, Selena, I know it's hard, and I know you are thirsty. We all are. But whimpering isn't going to speed things up. Just be patient." But this didn't seem to calm Selena down much.

"Tell you what, once the helmets are full, you can take my share of the water too, okay?"

Selena stopped whimpering on hearing this.

'That's my little sister! Always tough when she needs to be!"

It took a while, but finally the helmets were full and they could quench their thirst. The water tasted a bit salty, but it was still water.

When Selena finished her share, Blayt offered his. Selena drank a little, but left a good amount for Blayt. She did love her big brother after all.

They had to repeat the process of filling their helmets again to fully quench their thirst, but in the end they did.

But now came the other problem. Hunger. And there was no food around, anywhere, not even cave mushrooms. In the end they decided to just tough it out. If they were able to find water, hopefully they would find food soon enough. Only problem was, they didn't.

—◊◊—

CHAPTER 5

Rumbling

It had been at least a full day if not a little more since the friends had set out for their mission, and while they were able to get water whenever it was necessary, they still hadn't found any food. The last any of them had eaten was last night at dinner time (you have to remember that they'd left their homes without having breakfast). And now they weren't hungry, they were *famished*! It felt like their stomachs were sapping whatever energy they had left.

None of them had any strength left. Even standing was too much.

"Maybe we should head back. We've been walking for who knows how long, and we haven't found anything," said Jason,

"No. We are going to see this through to the end," said Loopa.

"Fine," said Jason.

Jason was so hungry, he didn't even have the energy to argue back.

Then Caprica started saying something but it just came out as a whisper.

"What was that Caprica?" asked Loopa.

Caprica forced herself to speak up. "I said, have you guys noticed that aren't any more stalactites?"

Now all of them stopped and really noticed.

"Hey, you're right," said Blayt. "I think the shaft has become bigger. Like there could be an echo!"

...like there could be an echo...like there could be an echo...like there could be an echo...

"I don't think we're in the shaft anymore," said Jason. "I think we are in a giant tunnel." He was right. They were in a huge tunnel. The ground was a bit rough, but weren't any more stalagmites. As for the stalactites, they were still there but now they were high enough not to bother them. The walls appeared to be completely smooth. Bizarre.

Looking back they saw a hole in the wall through which they had entered the tunnel. It was just that they were so tired and weak; they hadn't even noticed the change.

"Well, I think this is much better," said Selena, hunger half-forgotten for now. "I was getting tired of bumping into those pointy rocks."

"They're called stalagmites," said Caprica.

"Who cares?" said Selena.

"Well, this doesn't change things that much. We still don't know what's causing the earthquakes," said Loopa. "Let's move on."

"Wait a minute," said Jason.

"C'mon, Jason, staying isn't going to do us any good," said Loopa.

But he wasn't moving. In fact, on looking closer at him, he seemed to have a look of extreme concentration on his face.

"Jason?" said Caprica.

"Can't you fellows feel that?" asked Jason.

"What?" asked Blayt.

"I don't know. A kind of rumbling beneath my feet."

Now that he had pointed it out, they could feel something. And when they had all stopped talking, they could hear something too, coming from in front of them.

"What do you suppose it is?" asked Loopa.

"I'm not sure," said Jason.

"Ummm... fella's, I think we should move..." said Blayt.

"Why?" asked Loopa.

"Because that rumbling is getting louder really quick. And I'm pretty sure whatever's causing it is coming towards us."

Now the entire tunnel was shaking, above them the stalactites started swaying to and fro. They looked like they were going to fall any minute.

"You know what? I think we should move!" said Loopa.

"Good idea!" said Caprica.

And they all started running in the opposite direction.

They ran as fast as their feet would carry them, but they didn't last long. I had mentioned earlier how their hunger was half forgotten, but after running for a few minutes, they started to remember it again. Soon they started to slow down, and whatever was making the rumbling was getting closer.

Selena was the first to fall; it was just too much for the poor little girl. Call it an overdose of famishness. She had fainted.

Blayt immediately went back for her. As a result he was the first to see what looked like an enormous dust cloud headed their way. He froze, just for a second. But it was long enough for the dust cloud to catch up and engulf him.

Jason was the next to go. Now, only Caprica and Loopa were left. They held hands and ran, each trying to support the other. But soon enough the dust cloud had engulfed them too. But it was strange. Instead of being crushed, they were swept off their feet. They hung there in midair for a while, still holding hands, then they landed on something hard, that was moving, *fast*.

Have you ever slid down a slope filled with pebbles? Do you remember how you could feel the pebbles slipping under you? Loopa and Caprica felt something like that, but a little softer. Whatever it was it jostled them around a lot. And soon they were separated. Loopa could just make out that up ahead a smaller dust cloud seemed to be leaving the main tunnel and going into a smaller tunnel. And she seemed to be heading that way. After that, all the higgledy-piggledy of the entire day caught up with her, and even though she was being jostled around like a rag-doll, she, like Selena, fainted as well.

—∞—

CHAPTER 6

Granite and Obsidian

Loopa fell in and out of consciousness. When she was awake, she thought she heard people talking. "Are they okay?" "Who are they?" "What do they want?" was what she heard the first time she woke up. Then she passed out again.

The second time was just as strange. "They're humans!"

"Humans? What are they doing here?"

"Calm down."

"They....rest... we'll... later..." Then she was out again.

And the third time.

"They seem better."

"Give them some time. Then we'll talk to them."

"Hope they wake up soon."

Loopa finally woke up properly. She was lying down on the ground, inside what looked like a cave. Next to her, her friends were unconscious too. Or maybe they were asleep. Loopa raised her head a little, to get a better look. Blayt, Caprica and Jason were accounted for, but she couldn't see Selena.

She decided to get up. But the problem was that she was so stiff and in pain that just getting up felt like her bones were creaking like a door with rusty hinges. "Cre..e..e..ak!" went her bones as she slowly got up. Once that was done, she decided to get a better look at her surroundings. It was only now that she saw that the cave obviously belonged to someone. It seemed very clean and dust free, which was odd for a cave. There was light coming from the next room so Loopa made her way there. The room was large, and lighted by a strange plant which had leaves which glowed within the dark cave. In the middle was a slab of rock with big indentations around the edge. And further inspection showed a lot of decorations. A neat line of precious stones, what looked like a stone vase and a small indoor mushroom garden were just a few of the things she saw in this room.

"Slu..u..r..r..p!"

What was that? It sounded like it came from the slab with indentations.

Loopa turned her head back to the slab and saw that Selena was sitting there, cross-legged, eating something from out of one of the indentations.

"Cru..u..nch," went something in her mouth, then she looked up and saw Loopa.

"Loopa! You're awake! Come here. This stuff is really good. I don't know what it is, but it tastes really great!"

Loopa slowly made her way to the table (she realized that was what the slab of rock was supposed to be. The Indentations were probably something like plates) and took a seat next to Selena. Then she took a good whiff of whatever was on Selena's plate. It made her mouth water.

But she didn't want to eat just yet. First she had to find out what was going on.

"Selena, what happened? How did we get here? The last thing I remember was running, getting swept off my feet and landing on something hard which was moving."

"Well, we were saved," said Selena, still eating.

"By whom?" asked Loopa.

Then Loopa heard a shuffling nearby. She looked around to see what it was.

"By them," said Selena.

Loopa's jaw dropped in surprise when she saw who it was. No, it couldn't be.

"Looks like your grandma was right," said Selena.

It sure did. Standing on its four little legs, with its big tail swishing behind, big mouth in front, rocky sand like scales all over, right in front of Loopa's eyes was a bona-fide earth-croc.

The earth-croc was smaller than she thought it would be, and much less dangerous looking. Sure, it had sharp teeth like all crocodiles, but its face had such a gentle look. Anyone could see that at least this particular earth-croc wasn't dangerous at all.

"So nice to see you're finally awake, dearie," said the earth-croc, in a grandmotherly type voice. Now this was a surprise to Loopa. In all her grandmothers stories she never mentioned earth-crocs could talk, let alone be so nice to strangers!

"If you're feeling hungry, I have some more mushroom and beetle stew you can have."

Loopa made a face when she heard the word "beetle." The earth-croc must have noticed this, because then she said, "I know most humans don't eat insects, but they're full of protein and can be very tasty when cooked right. Besides, your friend doesn't seem to mind."

Indeed, Selena didn't seem to mind at all. She just went on eating the stew like it was the best food in the world. Slurp, crunch, slurp, crunch, on and on went Selena!

'Just try the stew dear, you don't have to take it if you don't like it," said the earth-croc. With that the earth-croc brought out a huge bowl of steaming stew. She used her nose to tip some of the contents into the nearest indentation, and gestured towards Loopa to have some.

Loopa hesitated. She wasn't so sure about the mushroom and *beetle* stew. But she *was* hungry and the stew did smell pretty good.

She decided to try some. She gathered up what she could in her cupped hands and slurped some of the stew in.

That was all it took. Now even Loopa was chowing down, just like Selena.

Loopa thought she should be polite and mention that she liked it. "It's delicious! Thank you ma'am."

"Call me Grandma-granite, and I'm glad you like it," said the earth-croc, smiling.

Once Loopa thought she had had enough stew, she wanted to ask some questions.

"I'm sorry Grandma-granite, but I have to ask, what happened to us? Where are we? How on earth did we survive?"

"All in good time, dearie, all in good time! I'll answer all your questions, but I think we should wait for all your friends to wake up; otherwise I'll have to start all over again. And, as it is, I'm getting slow in my old age. In the meantime, why don't you finish your stew?"

Loopa decided that Grandma-granite had a point. Might as well wait for the others to wake up and then hear the details. Besides, she was enjoying the stew.

"Thank you Grandma earth-croc... I mean, Grandma-granite."

"That's quite alright dear."

And so Loopa and Selena continued to chow down, and I must say that despite her size, Selena sure did eat a lot!

Once eating was over (and by now both of them felt that they'd never be able to move again), Loopa started questioning Selena. Selena told Loopa that she woke up and found Grandma-granite watching over her. At first Selena thought she was still asleep and dreaming, "But one I realized I was awake, I was about ready to scream, when Grandma-granite stated talking and calmed me down. Then she told me I looked like I hadn't eaten in days and she gave me some stew. I was eating that when you woke up."

Loopa was a bit disappointed that this was all Selena knew. But only a bit. Now that Selena had stopped talking, Loopa focused her full attention on Grandma-granite who was moving about, finishing whatever chores earth-crocs had to do. Loopa had only one thought going through her head, "they exist, they really exist!" But pretty soon Grandma-granite stated to feel uncomfortable at being stared at. So she decided to confront Loopa.

"I'm sorry dearie, but do you mind not staring at me like that? And if you must stare, at least tell me why?"

"Oh, I'm sorry! It's just...that..."

"Yes?"

"Well, my Grandmother used to tell me a lot of stories about earth-crocs, and I used to really believe her."

"Used to?"

"Yes. But recently I had stopped believing. And now, here you are, right in front of me, taking care of me and my friends, feeding us and... I just don't know what to make of it all. I guess it still hasn't settled properly in my head yet!'

Grandma-granite shuffled in one spot a little, trying to figure out what to say to this.

"Well, I suppose that can't be helped... alright dearie, if you think it helps, you can stare at me as long as you want, until it does settle in your head. But do try to hurry it along please. I do feel uncomfortable when someone stares, makes me wonder whether I have something stuck between my teeth, or some such similar thing!"

"No, no, you have nothing stuck in your teeth Grandma-granite." Loopa was really getting used to calling the old earth-croc that. "And you don't have to feel uncomfortable any more. I think it's settling down now, so I'll stop staring."

Grandma-granite gave a huge smile at this. At least Loopa thought it was a smile. She was showing more teeth anyway.

"Thank you, dearie. Now I had better get my chores done. Call me if you need anything. Or if your friends wake up."

So Grandma-granite dragged herself away to finish her chores.

—⟋⟋—

Loopa had to wait a long time for the rest of her friends to wake up, but they did wake, eventually.

First to wake up was Jason. Like when Loopa first met Grandma-granite, he too got a bit of a shock, then he talked to Loopa and Selena and, with them, waited for the others to wake up.

The process was repeated with Caprica when she woke up, and Blayt (except Blayt was more worried about his sister than anything else, "I'm fine, brother; please leave me alone, you're embarrassing me!").

Once they were all awake (and well fed) Grandma-croc finally told them what happened in the tunnel. Apparently, the crocs didn't notice the kids at first. It was only when the earth-crocs reached their village that they even realized that some of them had picked up some unwanted passengers.

Once the crocs realized that the passengers were human, there was a lot of hullabaloo and excitement and some panic too. The earth crocs hadn't seen any humans for years. They'd almost forgotten that humans even existed.

And now five of them just pop out from nowhere.

Who were they? How did they get here? Why were they here?

Who, what, why, how??

Eventually the crowd (by now a crowd had gathered) decided to ask them. But none of the humans would wake up.

Eventually Grandma–granite's grandson, Obsidian volunteered to keep the humans in his house and take care of them until they woke up. Then he would take them to the council and they could question them and figure out what to do with them.

"And then of course, Obsidian brought you here and he and I have been waiting for you to wake up ever since. And I must say, it is a real delight to see humans again. The last time I saw any humans, I was a young earth croc of 10."

But the children were not listening to Grandma-granite anymore. This was too much. Here they were, in the middle of what was probably an earth-croc village; they were curious and wanted to ask questions of their own, and they were the ones who were being questioned!

They were the ones who were supposed to give answers. How unfair was that?

"Um, Grandma-granite," said Loopa, "Would you mind leaving us alone for a little while? We would like to talk to each other. In private, please."

"Oh of course, dearie. Would you like to have something to eat while you talk?"

"No Grandma-granite. We don't want anything. We just want to talk."

"All right dear."

So Grandma-granite made her slow way out, leaving the children to talk.

However, once she had left, none of them even started talking.

Where should they begin?

Jason decided to try a start.

"Well this is a strange situation we've gotten ourselves into."

"THAT is an understatement," said Blayt.

"It's still hard to believe that the earth-crocs actually exist," said Caprica.

"Well, I'm glad they exist," said Selena. "It makes a nice change to know that some fairy tales might actually be true."

"That aside, we still have a problem," said Loopa. "While I *am* excited about the earth-crocs, we have to try and get this questioning business over and done with soon. After that, we still have to find out what is causing the earthquakes."

"Maybe we can use this situation to our advantage," said Caprica.

"What do you mean?" asked Loopa.

"Well, they are going to question us. Maybe in return, we can ask them some questions. After all, they might know about the earthquakes. Maybe it's harming them too. Then, maybe we could work together to stop the earthquakes."

The rest of the friends smiled at this. They liked the plan.

"It makes sense," said Loopa. "After all, who would know more about the earth than an earth-croc?"

"What if the earthquakes aren't harming them?" asked Jason. "They might not help us."

"You always have to look at the downside, don't you?" said Blayt.

"Hey! I'm just saying."

"It's still worth trying," said Selena

"All right then, we'll go to this council, answer whatever questions we can and then ask our own questions," said Loopa.

"And ask for help," said Selena.

"And ask for help," repeated Loopa. "So, are we all agreed?"

They all nodded, even Jason.

"Right, then. Grandma-granite, you can come back in now," said Loopa, raising her voice.

"Oh, that's good, I just finished baking the cookies," said Grandma-granite.

The 'cookies' of the earth-crocs were apparently a lot different from human cookies. They looked like lumps of coal with little crystals where the chocolate chips would have been.

"Umm, I'm not sure we can eat those," said Loopa.

This made Grandma-granite very sad. Most crocs loved her cookies.

"But they are very pretty looking," said Selena, seeing how sad grandma-granite looked. This perked up grandma-granite a bit, but she was still a sad.

So Jason (yes, Jason) decided to try the cookies. After all, the worst thing that could happen was that they would taste bad, right? In fact, they were very tasty, like sugar biscuits. The only problem was that they were rock hard.

"Well, Grandma-granite" (crunch), "I have to say" (crunch) "I have to say" (CRUNCH) "this is pretty good." (GULP) "It's just a little too..... well..... crunchy for my liking."

This at last, lifted Grandma-granite's spirits up.

"I could soften them up for you if you like."

"Could you? That would be very......."

"Actually, we wanted to talk to you," said Loopa.

"Oh!" said Grandma-granite slowly putting away the tray of cookies.

"We wanted to tell you that we were ready to meet the council," said Loopa. All of them got up, ready to continue their mission. But Grandma-granite had other plans.

"Oh, I'm sorry dears, but the council isn't ready to see you yet."

"What?" they all said together.

Their combined exclamations took Grandma-granite a bit by surprise. It took her a little while to recover.

"Well, dearies, my grandson is still out, informing the council about you."

"You mean they don't know we're here yet?" asked Blayt.

"No, and until he returns, I wouldn't advise you to leave. You'll be bombarded by other earth-crocs who would like to see you".

Now this was a strange turn of events.

"Well, what do we do until then?" asked Loopa.

"Softened cookies anyone?" asked Grandma-granite.

—⚏—

Everyone was rather enjoying the softened, coal black cookies. Especially Jason. Even Loopa was willing to put the mission aside for a little while as she had some more cookies. Only for a little while, though. As soon as they had finished eating, Grandma-granite's grandson, Obsidian came back.

"I'm home, Grandma!"

"Ah, welcome back young Obsi. Do come in here please."

An earth-croc came shuffling into the room. He was small and rather young looking, with large black eyes that shone like black crystals.

"Children, this is my grandson Obsidian. Obsi, these are Loopa, Caprica, Blayt, Jason and Selena."

"Hullo," said everyone.

"Hullo. I'm glad to see you're okay," said Obsidian.

'And we're glad to finally meet our rescuer," said Caprica.

This seemed to embarrass Obsidian a little. "It was nothing, really."

The friends took an immediate liking to the earth-croc. Anyone who was modest about saving others was okay with them.

"Well good friends, if you were worried about meeting the council you'll be happy to know that they are busy and so you won't have to meet them till tomorrow."

Now this was a disappointment. None of the friends were happy to hear this.

"But sir, we *wanted* to see the council. And soon," said Selena sadly.

"Oh," said Obsidian. "Well then, I'm sorry to be the bearer of bad news."

Well, this was just great. As it is, they had waited impatiently for Obsidian to arrive to take them to the council, and now they find out they will have to wait even longer!

"And by the way, you don't have to call me 'sir,' I'm not that much older than you," said Obsidian.

"Oh, I'm sorry. How old are you?" asked Selena.

"Sixty four," said Obsidian.

"But that is *very* old! My grandmother is sixty five."

"In human years it probably is old. But in earth-croc years I am very young. Grandma-granite is six hundred and fifty seven years old."

"I'll be six hundred and fifty eight this September."

Despite this, young Selena still thought of Obsidian as much older than even Loopa. Although she had to admit, he did look very young.

"I am very sorry for this turn of events," said Obsidian. "Let me make it up to you. Let me give you a tour of our village."

Loopa was not really in the mood for any sightseeing at that time. She was too disappointed.

"I'm sorry, but we're not in the mood right now."

"Are you sure?" asked Obsidian. "It's quite a wonderful place, and it will help pass the time."

"Well..."

"We might as well, Loopa," said Jason. "We have nothing else to do, after all."

"Besides, it could be very interesting," said Caprica.

"I want to see the earth-croc village!" said Selena.

"I second that," said Blayt.

It didn't look like Loopa had much of a choice. Besides, she thought it would probably be interesting too. After all, it wasn't every day you saw an earth-croc village.

"All right then, I third it," said Loopa.

"Yayy!" said Selena.

"Okay then, if you will all just follow me. Walk this way please."

"Will we have to shuffle like you?' asked Selena.

"Selena, don't be rude!" said Blayt.

"Ha, ha! No, no, you may walk whichever way you feel comfortable," said Obsidian.

"You all have fun. I'll have dinner ready for you when you get back," said Grandma-granite.

"Thanks Grandma," said Obsidian.

"Thank you, Grandma-granite," said Loopa.

And so they were off to see the earth-croc village, or town as some of the earth-crocs liked to think.

—m—

It was one of the most exciting and strange tours they had ever taken. The entire place was completely different from their village. To put it simply, it seemed to be a mixture of a rocky fortress and a mine.

Some of the earth-crocs had made their homes like stone igloos. Some had hollowed out the bigger stalagmites to make a pointy tepee. But most lived in large caves like Grandma-granite. None of the houses had a door or even a curtain in front of the entrances, just an open hole. Still, everyone seemed to respect each other's' privacy. Every few feet, they saw those strange trees with the glowing leaves, which lighted up the whole tunnel.

The children noticed that most of the caves were, like the mines, one on top of the other. But there didn't seem to be any stairs or ladders to go up or down. When asked, Obsidian pointed to some grooves at regular intervals on the walls, leading all the way to the top. "We use these to go up." Then he took them further down along the wall and showed them what looked like a giant rock slide. "And we use this to go down." The slide went all the way from the top of the wall of caves, till the bottom.

"I would like to go to the top and slide down!" said Selena.

"I wouldn't," said Jason.

"Neither would I," said Blayt. "And I'm not letting you either."

"Aww," said Selena. "Meany."

"It's quite safe, I use it all the time," said Obsidian.

"For an earth-croc maybe, but what about humans?"

"Hmm. You have a point," said Obsidian. "Well then, on with the tour."

Obsidian showed them a lot of things which were considered the pride and joy of the earth-croc village. The underground waterfall, the mushroom and insect farms, the biggest and smallest stalagmite house, the natural rock statues ("they have been like this when we found them. We never even touched them!") and even his school.

"And now I'll show you the place we're all most proud of. The earth-croc Running Station. It's the biggest station for miles around," said Obsidian.

By now the friends (even Loopa) had almost forgotten about their mission and had started really enjoying the new sites.

They were all looking forward to yet another earth-croc village marvel.

All that is, except for Blake. He had enjoyed himself a lot but as soon as Obsidian mentioned the running station, he suddenly remembered their mission for some reason. He also started to get the feeling that the station and their mission were related somehow and that their nice tour would come to a sad and bitter end. He didn't know how or why, it was just a feeling he had. A very strong feeling.

No one else seemed to notice Blayt's change of mood though; they were too caught up in their own thoughts.

Meanwhile, Obsidian was giving a running commentary. "The running station was made a little over a hundred years ago. Back then; this village was considered the centre of everything. It still is, even now, but there isn't as much glamour now as there was then. Back in the day, Grandma said it was almost impossible to move, the station was so crowded; especially during rush hour."

"Uh, excuse me, but what is a running station?" asked Caprica.

"Well, most earth-crocs travel (when we travel) in huge groups through the tunnel, at very high speeds. Running stations are places where earth-crocs can join or leave a travelling group or where the groups take a bit of a rest after a long days' running," said Obsidian. "In fact, now that you mention it, it was at the running station that we found you, on the backs of some of the earth-crocs of the last running group."

"Why didn't any of them notice us? You'd think a bunch of humans jumping around on earth-crocs' backs would be noticed immediately," said Jason.

"Well, you see, one of the problems with earth-crocs is that once we go into running mode, our brains tend to shut out a lot of things. You have to realize that since we live underground, earth-crocs always face the threat of cave-ins and what not, so we've developed rock like skins so we can't be harmed. Unfortunately, it also makes it hard for us to feel things that are not as hard as rocks."

"Lucky for us," said Loopa.

"Yes. Also, when we are in running mode, we don't notice anything but the crocs next to us and the destination. It's almost as bad as a stampede."

"Like I said, lucky for us," said Loopa again.

"Yes, sorry about all that but at least you weren't injured. That was lucky, don't you think?" said Obsidian "Anyway, about the running station....."

Selena was starting to get tired of this monologue and was just looking around when she finally noticed how disturbed her brother seemed.

"Are you O.K.?" asked Selena

"I'm not sure," said Blayt. "I just have a feeling."

"Oh!" said Selena, "What is it?"

"Well......" started Blayt.

"And here we are at the running station. Isn't it grand? A real sight!"

It certainly was big, huge even, but not what one would call grand. All it was, basically, was a big tunnel like the one the friends found themselves in before they were overrun by the earth-crocs. The only difference between the two was the fact that this tunnel had a kind of platform on the side for watching, with barriers here and there for lines and to stop spectator earth-crocs from accidentally falling off the platform.

"Well, what do you think?" asked Obsidian, who seemed to be very proud of this part of his village; he was probably expecting a lot of high praise and exclamations from the friends.

"Umm, it is..... very...... big," said Loopa.

"Yes," said Caprica, "quite large."

"Huge, even," said Jason.

"Oh!" said Obsidian, sounding a little disappointed at the lack of enthusiasm. "Well, it will get much better when you see it full, let me tell you. In fact," and Obsidian turned his head to his right, "I think a group of runners are coming right now."

That was when Loopa and the others felt a familiar rumbling beneath their feet. However, this was not like when they were in the tunnel. This was, to them, the warning signs of something they felt almost every day above ground.... the beginning of an earthquake.

"Obsidian," said Loopa, in a panic, "I think we need to get out of here. NOW!"

"Whatever for?" asked Obsidian.

"Can't you feel the earthquake coming?" asked Jason. The friends had already started moving quickly towards the entrance of the tunnel.

"What are you talking about?" said Obsidian. "Oh, here they come!"

A huge, thundering river of brown, white and yellow went past them. It was a large group and they were indeed moving very fast! All you could see was the occasional tail and sometimes, a head. Otherwise, they might have been flat rocks with feet, gathered in a huge dust cloud.

But what really caught the friends attention was what was happening while the earth-crocs ran. The entire place was shaking like it would fall apart. Loopa and her friends could barely stand; in fact they didn't. Three of them had already fallen down.

Obsidian didn't seem to notice anything strange at all, like, as if this happened every time a running group went by. Meanwhile the running group was slowly thinning out, and with that, the shaking started to decrease. And once the running group was but a large dust ball in the horizon, the noise and the shaking stopped completely.

"Well, there you have it," said Obsidian. "Now, that was definitely a sight to behold!"

"We didn't have to behold it," thought Jason, while helping his friends to get up, "we *felt* it!"

"What's the matter?" asked Obsidian, "You all look, well, shocked."

The friends *were* shocked, and with good reason.

Two things had just happened. One was that Blayt had finally realized why he had had such a bad feeling earlier. It was obviously his intuition warning him about this. Two was that all the friends realized that the first part of their mission was over. They had found out what was causing the earthquakes up above.

Now they had to face the second part of their mission. How to fix the problem.

CHAPTER 7

The Elder Crocs

"It's you!" exclaimed Loopa. "You and the other earth-crocs are causing the earthquakes in our village!"

The friends had rushed Obsidian back to Grandma-granites cave, saying it was very important that they talk, immediately and in private.

"What? No, that's not possible! We didn't, wouldn't do that!" said Obsidian.

"But you have, and you did," said Caprica. "Just in front of our eyes."

"What do you mean, just in front of your eyes?" said Obsidian.

"It's your running station," explained Caprica. "Whenever a group of earth-crocs run in the tunnels, they cause an earthquake up above. In fact, I think the running station may be directly underneath our village."

"But, but…. the shaking is just the after effects of when earth-crocs run so hard. It never harmed anyone," said Obsidian.

"Maybe, but it is harming us," said Blayt.

"Back above the ground, people are harmed everyday by the earthquakes. Sometimes people even get killed," said Loopa.

Obsidian became wide-eyed and seemed very badly shaken on hearing this.

"Killed. We……… we're killing you?" said Obsidian.

"Well, people very rarely get killed," said Selena consolingly. It made her very sad to see how badly shaken Obsidian was.

"Rarely is bad enough," said Jason.

Selena gave Jason a very angry look when he said this. Couldn't he see how badly this news was affecting the young earth-croc?

Grandma-granite wasn't faring much better. No one seemed to have noticed, but Grandma-granite had come to see who it was as soon as she heard people talking. As a result she had heard everything that the friends and Obsidian had said to each other. "Oh!...... Oh my!" said Grandma-granite.

Everyone jumped, startled a little when they realized there was someone else in the room with them.

"Is... is this all true?" asked Grandma-granite.

"Yes," said Loopa. There was no point in trying to sugarcoat it.

No one said anything else for a while. Everyone was trying to process what they had just found out. Besides, what else was there to say?

"My dears, you must try to understand. If......if we had known; if we had had a clue......." Grandma-granite stopped in mid-sentence. "We never would have knowingly harmed you dears. Please try to understand that."

None of the children could stand to see Grandma-granite in this state after all she had done for them.

"It's okay, Grandma-granite," said Jason, going up to her and trying to console the old earth-croc.

"Yes," said Caprica. "None of you knew about any of this. We ourselves did not know until just a few moments ago."

The children's consoling seemed to work; Grandma-granite calmed down for now.

"The only question right now is, what do we do next?" said Loopa aloud.

No one seemed to have an answer to that question.

"I'll tell you what you have to do" said Obsidian, a fierce gleam in his eye.

"What?" asked all the friends together.

"You have to talk to the elders. They're going to see all of you to ask you questions. You tell them about your journey, about what is happening above ground. Together, I'm sure you will come up with a solution," said Obsidian.

"That's a good idea," said Caprica, a little excited.

"Yeah, we could tell them about this," said Jason, "the earth-crocs seem to be a peaceful race."

"We *are* a peaceful race," said Obsidian.

"Yes, yes of course," said Blayt, "and then we could make some plans, to somehow stop all of this. And then......."

"No more earthquakes," said Selena, a little dreamily.

Things were starting to look up again and about time too.

"Alright, it's settled. We will talk to the elders, and we will solve all our problems one way or the other," said Loopa, taking authority.

Unfortunately, they still had to wait for tomorrow. They could not get an audience with the elders before that. What were they to do in the meantime?

"We could continue the tour if you like," said Obsidian.

"Thank you, but I think we've had enough of that for now," said Jason.

"Indeed," said Caprica.

"More than enough," said Blayt.

"Well then, how about some more stew for you youngsters to eat?"

"Ooh! Yes please," said Selena, always willing for good food, no matter what.

—⚬—

Of course, saying something one day, and doing it the next, are two very distinct things altogether. After all, the mission they were on was quite difficult, to say the least, and in the end, they were just children.

So, as the friends made their way to the official looking, and quite honestly, the most intimidating cave they had ever seen, they started to feel their age. Or, more specifically, their lack of it.

While from a distance, the Elder cave looked just like any other cave, as they drew nearer, they noticed the finer details. The entrance of the cave was covered with sketches of earth-crocs in various action poses.

"That, my friends," said Obsidian, "is a depiction of the more notable parts of our history."

It was true that the quality of the drawings was not so good, but their quantity was overwhelming. Even inside the cave, the walls were covered with similar sketches. Obsidian put it upon himself to explain the drawings.

"This sketch depicts when we built our first 'above-ground' building. This one depicts the largest earth-croc to be born. And this depicts one of the first great journeys."

"Umm... Obsidian, we're not really interested in a history lesson right now," said Loopa.

"Oh, I'm sorry, it's just my way of dealing with nerves," said Obsidian.

"It's okay, we're all pretty nervous right now, Obsidian," said Blayt.

They walked on for a while, until they came up to a cave entrance similar to the one in front of Grandma-granite's home, except bigger.

"Well, friends, this is it. Behind this await the elders," said Obsidian. Everyone was nervous, and no one really wanted to go in. But it had to be done.

"C'mon everyone, let's just get this over and done with," said Loopa.

They all held each other's hands and moved forward. But someone was missing. Suddenly Blayt felt a tug on his left hand. Selena had stopped, and behind her was Obsidian, still standing where he had been.

"Aren't you coming?" Selena asked Obsidian. He slowly shook his head in sadness.

"I'm sorry. But only those who are summoned are allowed to see the elders."

Selena didn't want to go without Obsidian. She had grown attached to the young earth-croc.

"Its okay, Selena," said Blayt, seeing his sister's distress. "We won't be gone for long." She took one last look at Obsidian before she went on.

"One thing I should mention before you go in," called Obsidian, from behind them. "Many have made the mistake of underestimating the elders. Please do not make that mistake." On that cryptic note, the friends went forward.

In they all went in, to see.... nothing. The room was empty.

Well, not quite 'empty.'

The room itself was medium sized, with three strange stone altars standing side by side. They were quite simple looking. One was a three stepped pyramid. The next was two stones standing upright, with a third stone balanced atop the other two. And the last one was three stones leaning against each other, like a three dimensional triangle. Beneath each altar was a statue of a wizened old earth-croc.

"Is this some kind of joke?" said Jason. "All they have here are some statues!"

"You don't suppose these statues *are* the elders?" asked Caprica.

"Are you crazy? How can these wrinkled old pieces of stone be alive?"

It was true. They looked nothing like the earth-crocs they had seen. Those earth-crocs had looked alive. These looked just like stone. To prove his point, Jason went up to one of the statues and knocked hard on its nose.

That was when one eye opened.

"Aaaah!" screamed Jason. The old 'statue' blinked twice, then opened its mouth and gave a huge yawn. "My, that was a refreshing nap," said the 'statue.' It looked around and took notice of the five startled human faces.

"Oh, you must be the human children we've heard about. So sorry, it's just that work can be very tiring, and we're not as young as we used to be." The wizened old 'statue,' who was obviously one of the elders, stretched a little.

The children could have sworn they could hear mini stone avalanches inside the old earth croc as he moved.

"Magma, Ignatius, do wake up please. We have guests."

Now the other two statues opened their eyes and stretched. The friends heard more mini-avalanches.

"What is it, Rubble? I was having a nice dream," said one of the recently awakened elders. Then he too noticed the human children. "Ahh, I see. So they've come."

The children were stunned; the three elders were like nothing they had ever seen before. Grandma-granite was old, but the elders, they were ancient!

They remembered something Obsidian had told them in passing. The older an earth-croc gets, the more like stone they become. The elders looked just like statues with eyes.

"When you're done staring at us, we would like to get to the reason we called you here," said one of the elders. The children snapped out of it, and felt very awkward.

Loopa decided to take the initiative (seeing as no one else would). "Umm... yes Sir. Well, umm, we would like to tell you something. You see..."

"Wait, young one," said Ignatius. "If it is all the same to you, we would like to speak first. Age before beauty you know."

This made Loopa annoyed. She didn't like being interrupted.

"Well, actually sir, what I have to say is impor.."

"Of course your honor, we understand completely," said Caprica, interrupting poor Loopa again.

"Very good," said the elder.

"What are you doing?" whispered Loopa.

"I'm trying to appeal to their better nature," whispered Caprica back. "If we let them talk first, they'll have to listen to us later."

She had a point. "Oh, alright," whispered Loopa.

"Right then. To business," said the elder, called Ignatius. "We can see that you too have something you wish to say, so we will only ask one question. We want you to answer it, and then you may speak as you wish."

The children nodded. It seemed fair enough.

"Very well. This is our question. Why have you come here, and how did you get here? Speak the truth now, we have ways of knowing if you lie. And we do not appreciate liars."

Now this was a strange coincidence. The answer to the elders' question was what they all wanted to say in the first place! Talk about lucky.

"Well sirs, this is how it is..." So the friends told the elders their story. Each of them told different parts of it. They told them about the earthquakes, their plan, the journey, meeting Grandma-granite and Obsidian, and, of course, their realization at the running station. "And so, we were hoping that maybe you could do something to help us," finished Loopa.

When it was over, each of them felt out of breath and a bit tired. That was one hurdle down, at least, but now they had to face the next one.

The three elders were deep in thought after the friends had finished talking. Loopa started to think that maybe they had fallen asleep again.

"This is a very interesting tale you've told us." Nope, they weren't asleep.

"In fact, it helps clear up something which happened long ago," said the elder.

"Oh?" said Loopa.

"Yes. You've told your tale, now it's our turn. You see, many years ago, our village and running station were at a different location. It was nice and big, and we all liked that place. But then, things changed. There were explosions, and stalactites started falling from the roof much more often than was usual. It became so bad that we *had* to move our *entire* village to a new area. Here. It was tough, but we accomplished our goal, nonetheless."

When the elder finished his tale the children wondered why he was telling them all this. It had nothing to do with them.

"Umm...Sir, not to sound disrespectful, but what was the point of that story?" said Jason.

"Well young one, after hearing your tale, we now believe that the cause of our discomfort so long ago was your kind," said the elder.

"What?" exclaimed Jason and Loopa, together.

"You see, the location of our old settlement is directly beneath you mines."

"Oh... oh dear!" said Loopa.

"Hmph. One could say that *you* have gotten your just desserts," said one of the earth-croc elders.

"Hey, that isn't fair," said Blayt.

"Yes Magma, what is the use of goading the children?" said the smallest earth-croc elder, Rubble.

"I was just stating my mind, nothing more," replied Magma.

"Hmph. You always were a hothead," said the elder.

Rubble turned back to the children. They had been awfully quiet, and in the elders' experience, quiet children were not usually happy children. "I think you wish to say more, do you not?"

"Well, yes we do," said Loopa.

"Then, please speak your mind."

"We wish to know what you will do about our problem, now that you know you are the cause of it."

"That... is a very good question. It is something we must ponder over," said the elder.

"If I may make a suggestion," said Caprica.

"Yes?"

"You could do what you did so long ago and change your location again," said Caprica.

Magma seemed to become very angry at this. He let out a loud snort. "You insolent pup! Why should we inconvenience ourselves for you? It took us more than a hundred years to make this village! Why don't *you* leave your comfy little homes? What goes around comes around, after all!"

"But that is our home," said Loopa. "You wouldn't *make* us leave, would you? It is not our fault, the mines."

"You made *us* leave, long ago," said Magma.

"You've hit the nail on the head, Sir. It was long ago," said Caprica. "Besides, do you really wish to punish us for what our ancestors have done?"

This seemed to calm Magma down a little. "I hate to admit it, but you do speak the truth. And, besides, it is in the earth-crocs nature to hold a grudge."

"Ha, ha! You could have fooled me," said Ignatius.

"If it is any help, we would never have gone on mining if we had known it was causing you harm," said Caprica.

All three elders were silent for a while. The children were starting to wonder what would happen now.

"You have given us much to think about, young ones," said the elder called Rubble. "We must debate amongst ourselves what is the best course of action. I would ask you to leave and wait outside while we decide."

"But it's obvious that the best choice would be for you to m..." began Loopa.

"We understand, Sirs," interrupted Caprica. "We will leave now." And out they went, Loopa a little reluctantly.

Well, there they were, outside the elders' office, playing the waiting game again.

When they had first come out, Obsidian had wanted to bombard them with questions, but each of them had looked so serious, he had decided against it. The tension in the outer room was so thick, you could probably cut it with a knife.

Finally it became too much for Obsidian. He had to ask. "Aarrr... what happened in there? What did the elders say? Will they help you? Won't they? Why are you all so quiet?"

"We're just worried, Obsidian," said Blayt, "About whether the elders will help us at all. Or will they just hang us out to dry."

"I'm sure they'll be fair," said Obsidian.

"Yeah, fair to themselves," said Jason.

"Now, now, don't be hasty," said Obsidian.

"Yeah, after Caprica's speech, I doubt any of them will say no," said Loopa. Caprica smiled a little on hearing this.

"Yes, Caprica's speech will save the day!" said Selena.

"I don't think so," said Jason.

"Oh, do be optimistic, Jason. We've gotten this far after all," said Loopa.

Then a voice came from the elders' room. "Children, please come on in. And bring your young earth-croc friend with you as well."

"What? Why do they want me there?" asked Obsidian, looking nervous.

"Let's find out," said Blayt.

They all went back in, this time with Obsidian bringing up the rear.

The elders had gone back to their earlier positions, and each of them looked serious. The friends felt a bit scared looking at those faces.

"After much talking and debating, we have made a decision."

Well, here it was, the moment of truth again. Would the friends quest end in failure or success? Every one of the children were holding their breaths and crossing their fingers, or, in Obsidian's case, claws.

"We have decided that we, the earth-crocs will find another place to make our running station, thus ridding those who live above of any and all hurt and discomfort."

The friends started cheering and shouting their heads off. Loopa and Caprica hugged, Jason started dancing around, Blayt picked up his sister and spun her around in a circle. Obsidian joined in the fun too. Selena even went up to the elders and gave each of them a kiss. Each of them was having their own little celebration. They had done it. They had done it!

"HOWEVER," said all three elders together, loudly. Uh, oh! This didn't look good.

"We are inconveniencing ourselves and our people greatly for you and your kind," continued Ignatius, "so you must do something for us in return."

Silence. The children waited with bated breath for what the elder might say.

"In return, you must, when you return home, spread the word of the existence of the earth-crocs. This problem occurred only because the world has forgotten us. You," the elder pointed his claws at the children, 'will remind them of our existence."

Well, that didn't sound too hard. Except, "if we are to spread the word of your existence, we would need proof," said Caprica.

"You could take my baby tooth," said Obsidian. "An earth-croc's tooth is the one thing which isn't like stone. It's quite unique. It would be perfect."

"Well then, we see no problem. What say you?" said Elder Rubble.

The children smiled at each other; this they could do.

"Just to be sure," said Jason, "as long as we do this for you, you will change the whole running station?"

"You have our word."

All the children looked at each other and back to the elders, and said at the same time, "we accept!"

"Then it's settled," said Rubble. "Now, Obsidian, would you do us the favor of helping these children find their way home, once they are ready?"

"It will be my honor."

"Then you may leave. We have much to attend to, as you can imagine," said the elder.

"Yes sirs," said Loopa, "and we thank you very much."

"Can anyone remind me which ones are stalactites and which stalagmites?" asked Selena.

They were back in the tunnel again, making their way back to the mines. The only difference was, this time they had a guide. Obsidian was proving a very good guide and a good friend too. He even volunteered to carry Selena on his back during the journey. They had promised each other that if they could, they would see each other again.

But now they had more pressing matters to think about.

"You do realize that once we get back, our parents are going to be furious with us," said Jason.

"That's it Jason, keep reminding us of more worries," said Blayt.

"Yes, try to be more optimistic please! After all, we've done so much good. Thanks to us, and to the earth-crocs too (this to Obsidian), the whole village will never have to face earthquakes again," said Caprica.

"And also, once this blows over, and our story gets out, we'll be considered heroes," said Loopa.

"And we even got a friend out of it," said Blayt.

"Alright, alright, you're right, we did pretty good. The earthquakes are finally over," agreed Jason, for a little while showing his lighter side. "But our parents will still be furious!" And back to his darker side.

"Hmm," said Blayt. "At least Selena is enjoying herself."

"So, Loopa, what are you going to do now?" asked Caprica.

"Well, once the excitement is over, I think I'm going to finish that sandcastle," said Loopa.

"Hey, c'mon, you're being left behind!" called Selena, who was indeed very far ahead.

"We're coming, we're coming," said Blayt.

And so they all went forward, back to their now earthquake free lives. Back to just plain fun and relaxation. And, of course, back to getting scolded by their parents. But hey, they didn't seem to mind!

THE END

WRITER'S BIO

Avinash Sen was born in Manchester, England, in 1990. When he was four years old, his parents moved with him, back to his home country, India, where he grew up in the small town of Jabalpur. After completing his schooling, he moved to Kuala Lumpur. He is now a student (of Interactive Media) in Kuala Lumpur, Malaysia.

The writer is dyslexic, and started to read and write when he was 10 years of age, but his disability has never held him back and writing remains his first passion. Apart from writing, his other interests are reading, making videos and browsing through bookshops.

His first publication is an e-book called "What a Scythe" available on Amazon.

Printed in the United States
By Bookmasters